For my beloved Calvin, along with my wonderful nieces and nephews—B. M.

To Richard and Chris—I will ever be grateful for your trust and friendship—B. D.

Visit us at ShadowMountain.com

Library of Congress Cataloging-in-Publication Data

Mull, Brandon, 1974– author.
Pingo and the playground bully / Brandon Mull ; Brandon Dorman, [illustrator].
pages cm
Summary: When Chad and his friends hold a competition to see whose imaginary friend is the best, the schoolyard bully says his is the best, but in the end everyone learns the true power of friendship.
ISBN 978-1-60907-178-3 (hardbound : alk. paper) [1. Friendship—Fiction. 2. Bullies—Fiction. 3. Imaginary playmates—Fiction.] I. Dorman, Brandon, illustrator. II. Title.
PZ7.M9112Pk 2012
[E]—dc23 2012017332

Printed in Mexico 7/2012
R.R. Donelley, Reynosa, Mexico

10 9 8 7 6 5 4 3 2 1

PINGO

and the Playground Bully

Written by Brandon Mull

Illustrated by Brandon Dorman

SHADOW
MOUNTAIN

In second grade, Chad often played with his imaginary friend, Pingo, during recess.

Several of his classmates had imaginary friends as well.

Gary protected the galaxy with the help of his robot, Sparky.

Tiffany helped save the day with Awesome Girl.

And Dustin could hide

Mr. Bob in his pocket.

Sometimes Chad and his friends went adventuring together.
They battled lunch-meat creatures from the cafeteria.

Other times they hunted the fierce

Yard-duty-osaurus.

ROSIE
WAS HERE

Occasionally, they had to run from a bully named Jeremy and his imaginary pal,

GRUNT.

One recess, after defeating a clan of lava monsters, Chad and his friends began to argue about who had the best imaginary playmate.

"Sparky is best because he's the smartest," Gary declared.

"Awesome Girl is best because she's the strongest," Tiffany claimed.

"Mr. Bob is best because he's the sneakiest," Dustin maintained.

"Pingo is best because he's the coolest," Chad asserted.

The kids decided to hold a competition to prove which imaginary friend was best.

Chad noticed that Pingo didn't seem very excited. "Don't worry," Chad said to his friend. "You can beat those guys."

"This is silly," Pingo said. "Contests only prove who is best at certain things."

"We can't back out now!" Chad exclaimed. "They'll think we're scared!"

"I'll try my hardest," Pingo said.

Sparky won the spelling and math competitions.

Pingo came in second.

Awesome Girl won the athletic competitions.

Pingo came in second.

Mr. Bob won the hiding and spying competitions.

Pingo came in second.

“Our friends all won a competition,” Gary bragged. “It might take more contests to decide the true champion, but it looks like we already proved who is second best!”

“What is Pingo anyway?” Tiffany asked Chad.

“He’s a mix of things,” Chad replied. “And he’s got the best imagination here!”

“Then maybe he should have imagined better abilities,” Dustin pointed out.

Just then, Jeremy and Grunt launched a surprise attack,
pinning Chad and his friends into a corner.

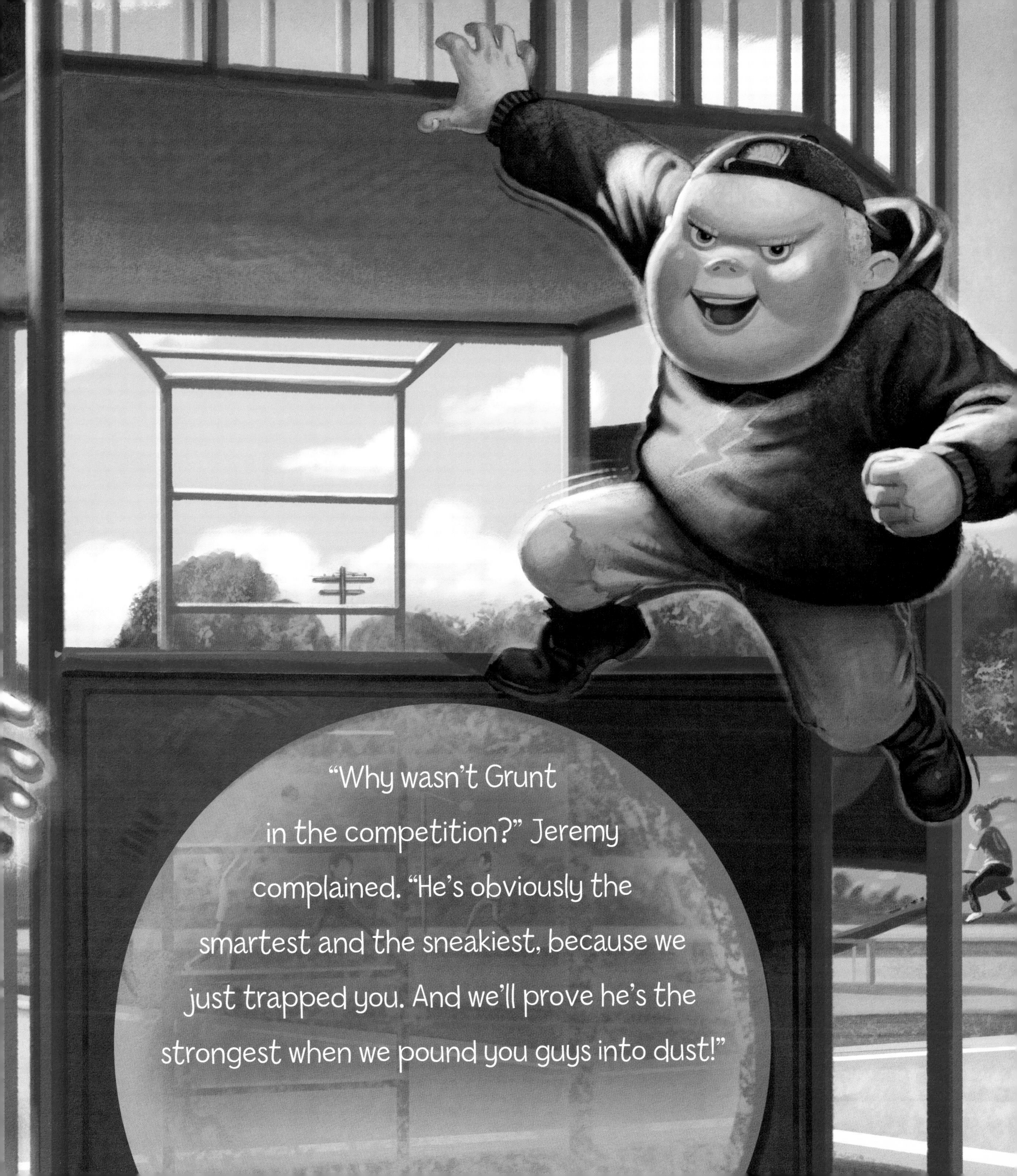

"Why wasn't Grunt in the competition?" Jeremy complained. "He's obviously the smartest and the sneakiest, because we just trapped you. And we'll prove he's the strongest when we pound you guys into dust!"

Chad and his friends were terrified. Sparky started to overheat and malfunction. Awesome Girl flew off to hide. And Mr. Bob slipped into Dustin's pocket.

Then Pingo stepped forward. "We would have loved to have had you in the contest, Grunt! I bet you would have won most of the medals. We can do another one next week. Right now, we're starting a new game.

"Want to come on an adventure down the Amazon River with us?"

"I've never been on a river trip," Grunt said.

"We could use your help," Pingo replied. "It will be risky, with giant snakes, native warriors, and rival explorers, but we might find the lost city of gold."

ADIE
CHASE
9
8
7
6
5
4

"You really want to play with us?" Jeremy asked.

"Sounds like fun," Grunt said.

"The playset can be the boat," Chad suggested.

"We'll go get the gear ready," Grunt and Jeremy offered.

"Pingo saved the day!" Gary cheered.
"Pingo is the bravest!" Tiffany shouted.
"Pingo is the most fun!" Dustin yelled.
"Pingo is the best!" they all agreed.

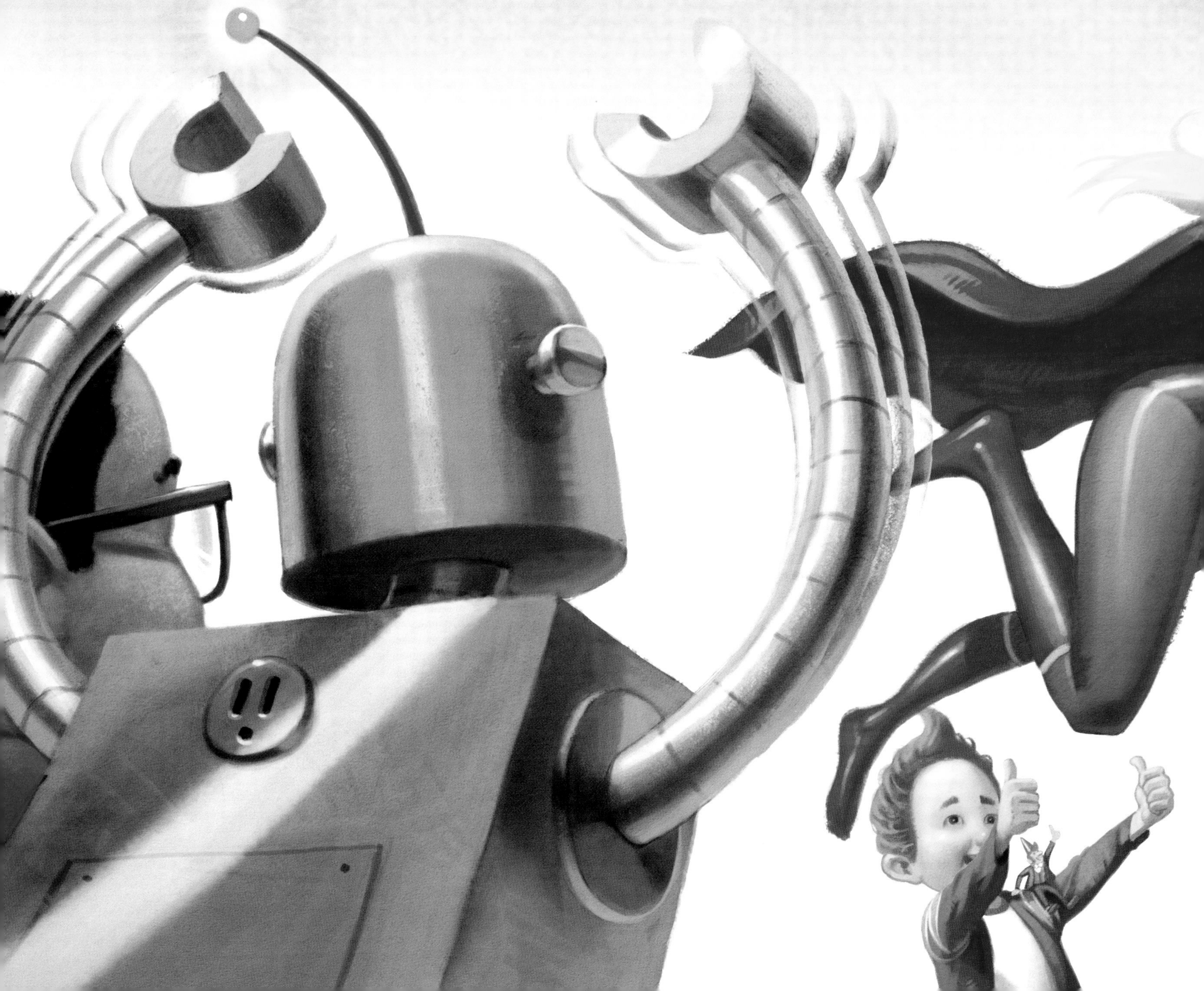

“Thank you, but this is silly,” Pingo said. “Nobody is the best. We’re all good at different things. And that makes friendship fun.

“Let’s go play!”

And so began a fresh adventure with a new friend.